For Granny Jill, who always took me to feed the 'bords',
and Trish, who helped me find the room to write this book – JB

For my grandchildren –
Saskia, the inspiration for bird girl,
and Marlo, Hemi, Ivan and Tomi – EW

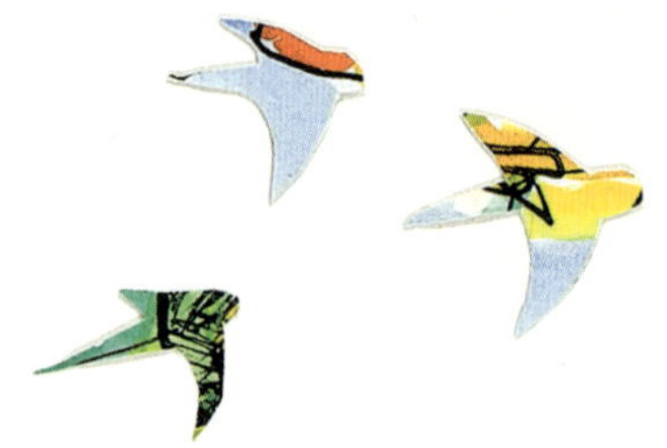

This book was inspired by Emily Dickinson's most famous poem
"Hope" is the thing with feathers, which starts:

"Hope" is the thing with feathers –
That perches in the soul –
And sings the tune without the words –
And never stops – at all –

We began working on this book in 2019 after bushfires ravaged much of Australia's east coast. Horrified by the impact the fires had on the wild places we love, we wanted to create a work that speaks to the many ways hope presents in the world. For us, hope isn't just an eagle soaring in a cloudless sky. It's also the ibis raiding bins.

The girl in this book pays close attention to birds and uses her observations to create an imagined world filled with art and hope. This little girl is us and we also hope she is you!

www.johannabell.com | www.ericawagner.com.au

This book was written in Garramilla (Darwin) on the land of the Larrakia and illustrated in Naarm (Melbourne) on Wurundjeri land. We pay our respects to Elders – past, present and emerging – and to First Nations storytellers everywhere.

Hope is the Thing

Johanna Bell & Erica Wagner

ALLEN&UNWIN
SYDNEY • MELBOURNE • AUCKLAND • LONDON

Hope is a kookaburra

singing the sun

Hope is the emu learning to run

Hope is the wedgetail
soaring high
Hope is a grass owl
nesting nearby

Hope is a seagull
eyeing off chips
Hope is the hollow in a eucalypt

BARTON
Aggie
Gap
Franklin
Bendora
Dam
Manuka

Hope is the dash
past magpie's nest
Hope is a feather
from night parrot's chest

Hope is a song
on a moonlit mound
Hope is a secret
tightly bound

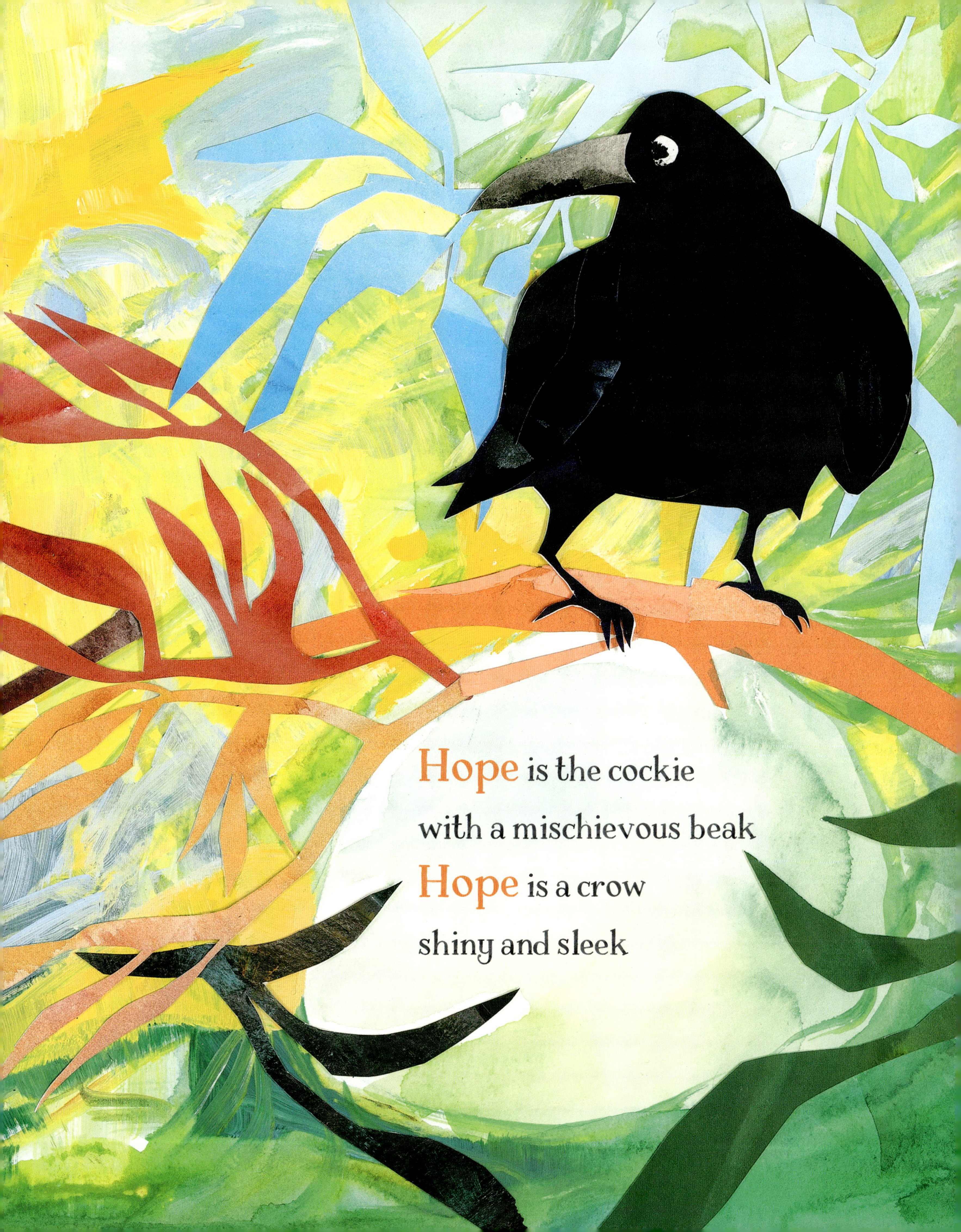

Hope is the cockie
with a mischievous beak
Hope is a crow
shiny and sleek

Hope is an albatross
taking off
Hope is the dance
of the white-winged chough

Hope is a curlew
migrating south
Hope is the squawk
of an open mouth

Hope is a pelican
patrolling for scraps
Hope is the pardalote
harvesting sap

Hope is the seed
in the palm of your hand
Hope is a footprint found in the sand

Lakesland
Thirlmere
Couridjah
Buxton
Balmoral
Yanderra
Hill Top
Alpine
HUME
HWY
Bargo
Tahmoor
Picton
Maldon
Mt Burke
Nepean Reservoir
Avon Reservoir
Avon River
Cordeaux River
Wilton
Broughton Pass
Mount Keira
Mount Kembla
Balgownie
Mulgoa
Wallacia
WESTERN
Emu Plains
North Springwood
Upper Castlereagh
Castlereagh
Cranebrook
Jamison Town
Orchard Hills
Penrith
Kingswood
St Marys
Werrington
Marsden Park
Grose Wold
Grose Vale
Agnes Banks
Windsor
Richmond
North Richmond
Kurmond
The Slopes
Tennyson
Freemans Reach
East Kurrajong

Hope is the bowerbird
hunting for blue
Hope is a red-tailed black-cockatoo

Hope is an ibis
raiding bins

FERNTREE
Clayton North
HUNTINGDALE
RD.
Oakleigh East
Holmesglen
Darling
Malvern
MALVERN
RD.
BALACLAVA
GLENHUNTLY
Gardenvale
BOUNDARY
GOVERNOR
East

Hope is the thing

with feathers and wings

ACKNOWLEDGEMENTS

So many people have helped us jointly and individually in the making of this book. Thank you to everyone who was part of the 2019 Octopus Story Camp, where the seed was planted. Thank you, Anna, for loving our vision from the very start; Grace, for backing us; Margrete and Craig, for invaluable art direction; Sophie, for shepherding our work with such care; Jo, for your flawless design; Toby, for your poetry insights; the team at Allen & Unwin, for all your seen and unseen work; and all our friends and family, for all the ways you've supported us: we made this book for you.

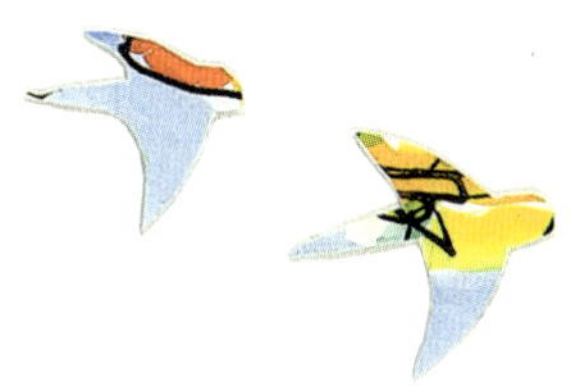

ILLUSTRATOR'S NOTE

The pictures in this book are mixed media collages on paper. Backgrounds are painted with watercolour, acrylic, gouache and ink. The collage elements include bits and pieces of old artwork, painted paper in various colours and tones, monoprints created from leaves, plain coloured paper, and fragments from two books: *The Australian Book of the Road*, published by Paul Hamlyn Pty Ltd, 1971; and *Encyclopaedia Britannica, Volume 3 – Baltimore to Braila*, published by Encyclopaedia Britannica Inc, William Benton, Publisher, 1962. Everything is glued down with binder medium or glue sticks, and occasionally Blu-Tacked for a 3D effect. Special thanks to Craig Smith for his Photoshop wizardry and so much else.

First published by Allen & Unwin in 2023

Allen & Unwin
83 Alexander Street
Crows Nest NSW 2065
Cammeraygal Country
Australia
Phone: (61 2) 8425 0100
Email: info@allenandunwin.com
Web: www.allenandunwin.com

Allen & Unwin acknowledges the Traditional Owners of the Country on which we live and work. We pay our respects to all Aboriginal and Torres Strait Islander Elders, past and present.

A catalogue record for this book is available from the National Library of Australia

ISBN 978 1 76118 002 6

For teaching resources, explore
www.allenandunwin.com/resources/for-teachers

Cover and text design by Jo Hunt
Set in 26 pt Little Mo by Jo Hunt

Colour reproduction by Splitting Image, Wantirna, Victoria

This book was printed in August 2024 by
C&C Offset Printing Co. Ltd, China.

10 9 8 7 6 5 4